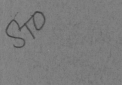

Rufus Gideon Grant

Rufus Gideon Grant

by Leigh Dean

Illustrated by Paul Giovanopoulos

Charles Scribner's Sons / New York

To *Keene* who opened the door
and
To *Earkis Hill* a Georgia sharecropper from 1928 to 1934

Rufus Gideon Grant sat on an old tree stump under a hot June sun, watching. Around him, on all sides, spread a tall, grassy field. He knew this field, its dips and swells, and this hard, flat-topped stump as well as he knew his own feet—and he'd been studying them for years.

Watching wasn't something you could hurry up. Sometimes, like now, when there wasn't much to watch, time went slow. And Rufus found his eyes just naturally fixed on his feet.

He liked the looks of his feet. He liked their lean, long look and the way the veins stood out—especially in the heat. And when he wiggled his big toe, the great tendon rose up under the skin like a mole's burrow, stretching from his toe over the top of his foot all the way to his ankle. Once he'd seen a picture in his history book that showed this statue of a boy whose name was David. The first thing he noticed was David's feet; they looked just like his.

A honeybee lit on his foot to wash its head. Rufus held his foot very still. Another honeybee passed by. And another and another, making the rounds of clover

blossoms, poking their long tongues into the tiny flowers, searching for nectar. Rufus watched the bees rising, banking, hovering, then sinking onto a blossom, every bee going about his own business.

I wonder if they knows each other? Rufus asked himself. *Or if they be friends? Maybe they-all lives in the same hive . . . I wish there was school.*

Every year when school quit for the summer, he felt the same. Yesterday, the last day of school, was no different. The bus slowed to a stop. The doors opened. He got off. The doors shut behind him.

Yesterday, as the bus drove away, he caught his last sight of Mr. Snyder, and waved. Then he saw some of the kids in his class pressed up against the large rear window, waving their goodbyes.

He had watched the orange bus until the speck of it disappeared into the flat, dusty distance. Then he had turned for home. Inside himself, he felt empty. Even the long walk home along the soft, silty, red clay path, which he usually liked, hadn't helped. And the emptiness inside him had deepened.

Now, until school began again in September, there would be no more foggy, early-morning bus rides along the deserted highway. There would be no more Jimmy Allen telling him about the way his black mollie ate up

all her tiny babies in his fish tank. There would be no more Loretta Ginsberg tickling him in the lunch line and whispering her wet, giggly secrets into his ears. And there would be no more Nathaniel Snyder.

Yesterday had been Mr. Snyder's last day, too. "I've been transferred to another school." That's what he told Rufus. And Rufus knew at that moment that he'd never find another teacher like Mr. Snyder.

He remembered the day they had met. Late October it was. That morning, he woke up to the heavy drumming of rain. For a little while he kept his eyes closed listening to the tinny sound of the rain on the roof and the louder *pit, pit, pit* sound of raindrops hitting the wooden planking close to the bed.

He didn't make a move to get up. His body felt so tired, and besides, his mama's large, heavy arm lay across him. It was the only thing between himself and the floor—his place in bed being the outermost edge on the right-hand side. He and his mama lay like two spoons, front to back: he, curled around the edge of the straw mattress and she, curled close around him. On the far side of his mama, Rufus could hear his father's slow, steady sighing. It was very hot and sticky lying there, and the bed smelled strongly of dampness and sweat.

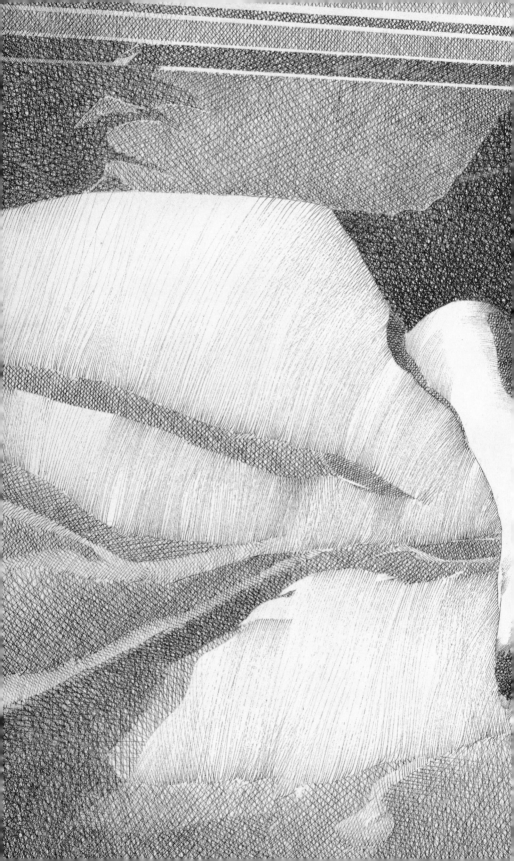

He opened his eyes. The shack was dark, as dark as night. Maybe it was night. But it felt like morning.

"Mama," Rufus whispered, "what time is it?"

"Hush child. Go back to sleep," whispered his mama.

"But Mama, if it's morning, I got school."

His mama groaned and raised herself up. "Well, go on. Get up an' look at the clock. But be quiet 'bout it."

Rufus held his breath and eased himself as quietly as he could off the bed. It was no use, though. Every bed spring his weight touched gave a low, rusty moan.

"Lazy good-for-nothin' . . . Anna, keep that boy still."

His father's voice rang out, and Rufus froze in the middle of the twilight room.

"The boy got school, U.L. Ain't no harm meant. I got to get up, too. Fix us some coffee. You stay restin', hear? Mr. Winthrup say he not comin' for you till noon."

Mr. Winthrup. That's why no one's up, thought Rufus. *They be takin' the week's cotton an' peanuts to the commissary today.*

Rufus found the old, battered clock with its face as big as his. The hands read seven-thirty. His heart be-

14

gan to pound and his stomach began to flutter. He got his shirt and shorts on in a hurry, and sat on the floor to pull on his high-topped sneakers. He was late, too late to catch the seven o'clock bus. He would have to walk, walk the eight miles to school. His books. He couldn't take them eight miles in the rain. He'd have to leave them home.

Just as he got to the door, his mama stopped him. "Rufus. You ain't even had your coffee. You ain't goin' out in that mess on an empty stomach."

"I has to, Mama. I be late."

The cool outside air hit him as soon as he opened the wooden door. He pushed out the screen door and stepped off the porch right into a muddy, ankle-deep puddle of water. The next instant he was drenched. Rivelets of water ran through his hair and down his face. His shirt and shorts stuck to his skin like wet paper sticking to a straw, and his feet began to squish inside his sneakers.

Bowing his head into the wind and squinting his eyes against the rain, Rufus set off for school. It was slow going. Every time he took a step forward he slid two steps backward. Finally, he broke into a jog to the chant, "Wet Georgia clay /Like a high stack of hay . . . Damn!" said Rufus, as he felt his ankles give way and twist under him. "The next slip-slide I take, I is sittin' right down to rest, even if it be in a puddle."

He hobbled along the cross country path for ten more hop-skip-slides and was really ready to plop into the mud when he looked up. Not twenty feet away lay the highway with its beautiful, hard, smooth surface. *Six more mile to go*, Rufus said to himself.

Down the highway he walked; he was the only traffic moving in either direction. Six miles later, he reached the branch-off that took him to the left down a dirt road to the big asphalt parking lot past the now swampy sports field to the back entrance of the sprawling, red-brick Booker T. Washington school.

Rufus figured the eight miles had taken him three hours. Long enough for the rain to stop and the sun to blaze forth, sending up vapors of steam from the earth and turning the playing field into a sparkling lake.

Rufus paused a minute by the wide, double-door entrance, then decided to stay outside. "I be that late already. No sense goin' inside to drip."

He made his way to the east end of school and, leaning himself against the building, closed his eyes and let the warmth of the sun begin to bake him dry.

As he stood under the bright heat, his hands behind him, pressing into the rough bricks, he felt a great tired-

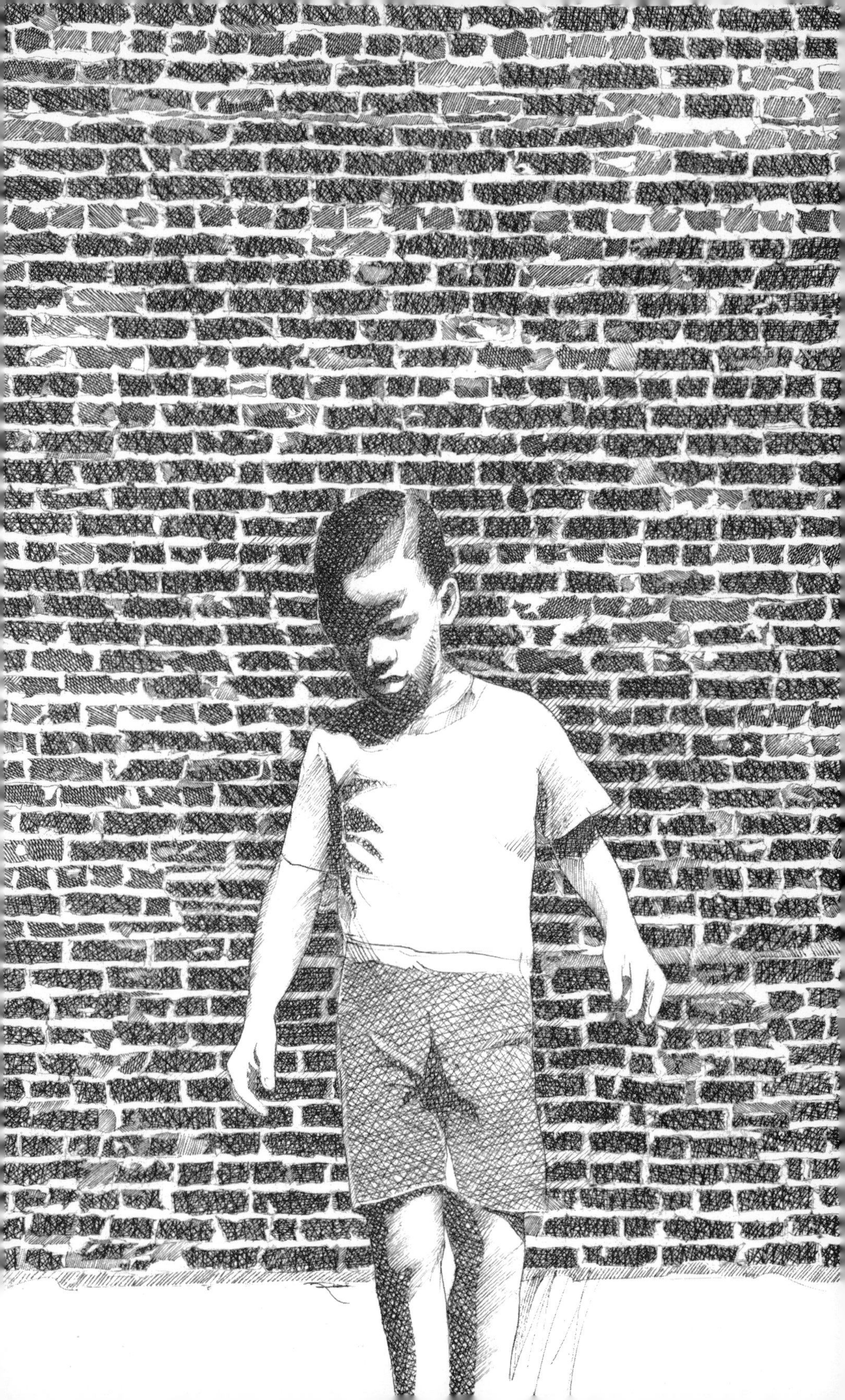

ness come over him and he wanted so badly to sit. To let his body slip down the side of the school and his head fall forward onto his chest.

Sleep, sleep, sleep, said Rufus's mind over and over. And he let his knees sag a little and his head nod forward. *Wonder if anyone be watchin'. Out a window maybe. Don't suppose so. They havin' that spellin' bee. Practice. P-R-A-C-T-I-C-E. Hesitate. H-E-S-I-T-A-T-E. Separate. S-E-P-A . . . got to remember they is "a rat" in "separate." S-E-P-A-R-A-T-E. Sleep.*

Rufus was almost asleep when the screech of a nearby window being raised brought him to. He turned and looked up. *Nothin' and nobody there.* He worked his way along the wall to the south corner and peeked around.

There came one grown-up trousered leg out the second story window followed by a backside and the other leg. Rufus watched in amazement. The shoe-covered feet felt for toe holds in the cement cracks between the bricks, and the legs lowered themselves down the side of the building. Five feet off the ground, the shoes pushed out from the wall and the whole body came out the window, landing with a thud, facing Rufus.

The man straightened up, brushing his hands to-

gether. Then he saw Rufus, staring at him, his mouth hung open, and the man threw his arms up over his head. "Caught me," he said. And Rufus found himself looking deep into a pair of serious black eyes that looked out at him from beneath a wide, bony brow. It was a thin, clean-shaven face. A wise and gentle face.

"You won't tell on me now, will you? I don't know how I'd begin to explain things to Mr. Espy."

Mr. Espy. Rufus collected his wits. *If he know the principal, he can't be no thief.* Then out loud Rufus asked, "You a teacher?"

"Yessir, I am. I'm Nathaniel Snyder, the biology teacher."

"Oh," said Rufus.

"You know," continued Nathaniel Snyder, "grades 9 through 12."

"Oh," said Rufus. "I'm only in the 4th."

"What are you doing out here?"

"Gettin' dry," Rufus answered. "I missed the bus an' walked in the rain. What you doin' out here?"

"I'm on my way to see about some baby rabbits." And Nathaniel Snyder started off toward a distant patch of scrub pine.

Rufus tagged along. "Can I come, too?"

"Are you dried out yet?"

Rufus felt his soggy shorts. "Nope."

"Come on, then. But I've got to hurry. Have to be back in time for fifth period."

Rufus ran to catch up to Nathaniel Snyder, then matched him stride for stride across the sloppy field.

They were halfway to the pines when Rufus found his tongue. "I know somethin' 'bout rabbits."

"You keep tame ones?"

"Nope. Wild ones. Marsh rabbits."

"It's a marsh rabbit's family I'm going to see about. A dog came in with a female two days ago, and by the looks of her she was nursing a litter. Thought it might be the ones out by the scrub pine."

"Were she dead?"

"Yes, she was dead."

"Oh."

Underfoot, the stubbly grass of the mowed field gave way to a soft, wet mat of pine needles. And overhead, the strong glare of the sun got weaker as it splintered itself on the crowns and branches of the trees. In among the pines, it was shadowy and cool.

Mr. Snyder stopped. Half hidden in a snake-like tangle of roots was the black opening to the rabbit's nest. And near the opening, two soaked lumps of brownish fur huddled together. Mr. Snyder stooped over and

touched the babies to see if they were alive. The rabbits
squeezed closer together.

"These two will make it," he said with satisfaction.

Rufus said nothing. He pulled his T-shirt off over
his head and knelt beside the rabbits. Gently, he lifted
first one and then the other on to his shirt.

"Here, use this to dry them," said Mr. Snyder, giving Rufus a large white cotton handkerchief.

Working from the head, down the back, to the belly and the legs, Rufus took the handkerchief and made the cleaning motions he knew the mama rabbit would have made if she were here to lick them with her tongue. Through the cloth, Rufus could feel the sharp outline of each tiny bone and he could feel the heart fluttering in the chest. Except for an occasional twitch of an ear and the stretching of a hind leg, they lay quiet under his stroking and did not try to get away. The eyes were not yet open, but the gummy mouths opened, and Rufus gave each baby a short suck on his little finger.

"Rabbit families mostly come in threes and fours." Mr. Snyder was on his hands and knees peering down the hole. "Better wrap those two up good and warm, then stick a hand down the burrow. There might be more. My hands are too big, now."

Rufus nodded. He got his shoulder as close to the hole as he could. Then, reaching in with his right hand, he felt along the dirt tunnel until his arm could stretch no further. He felt for side tunnels, and found one. It ended in a round pocket. At the bottom of the pocket, his fingers touched fur.

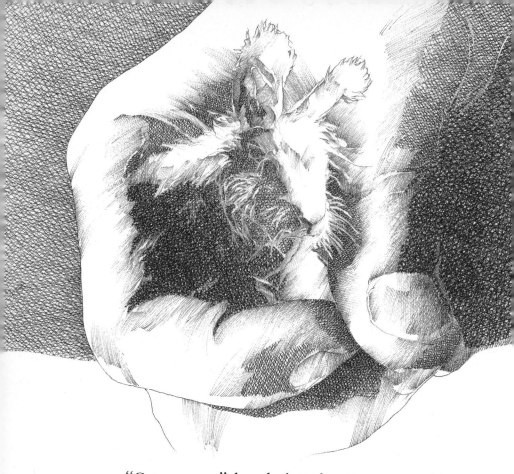

"Got me one," breathed Rufus. But even as his fingers closed around the ball of fur, he knew. He looked up at Mr. Snyder. "It be dead."

"The rain must have drowned it. Probably was the runt and didn't have strength enough to get out."

"I'll leave it be. It's a good grave," said Rufus. "I'll close it up with a stone." He found a large, flat stone and laid it over the hole. Then he made a small cross out of two sticks tied with a weed and stuck it into the ground at the head of the stone. Then he stepped back to see how it looked.

"We saved these two, anyway," said Mr. Snyder, cradling the babies in the crook of his arm. "Time I got back to school. You coming?"

"Yeah," said Rufus. Then, "Who's gonna take care of them?"

"Why, you and I are. Who else? I've been saving a box for just such a need. We'll put some grass and cotton in it and make another nest."

"We got to feed them, too."

"There're plenty of eye droppers in the lab and I'll get a carton of milk from the cafeteria. We'll put a little in a saucepan and heat it over a bunsen burner. Sometimes a science lab comes in handy. A made-to-order kitchen."

"Can I feed them?"

"You got yourself a job. Say, you know something?"

"What?"

"I never did ask you your name."

"It's Rufus. Rufus Gideon Grant."

They were nearly to the asphalt parking lot.

"Well, Rufus. Look. I'll give them the first feeding while you get along to class. Then during lunch hour you come to my room and take over. How's that?"

"Mmmm. Okay."

"Tonight I'll mix up a special formula, add some glucose and water to the milk, make it set better on their stomachs. You meet me here first thing in the morning to feed them. Okay?"

"Okay."

They arrived at a side door.

"Ain't you goin' in through the window?"

"No." Mr. Snyder smiled widely. "I only use the window to leave by. It gives me a chance to get some air and do some thinking—and no questions asked. Take care, Rufus. See you lunch hour."

That's how it had all begun that late October morning. For a time, the rabbits' feeding schedule gave Rufus an excuse to see Nathaniel Snyder every day. But the day came when they had to take the rabbits, grown big and strong, back to the pines.

All the way across the field, Rufus walked in silence. *What's I gonna do now . . . what's I gonna do now?* he asked himself again and again. *Here's this man I can't wait to see from one time to the next an' I prob'ly won't see him no more. I mean what's a twelfth grade teacher want a fourth grade kid hangin' around for?*

Mr. Snyder put down one rabbit. Rufus put down the other rabbit. And together they watched the rabbits

sniff the air, sniff the ground, then hop, hop, hop off into the scrub.

"We did a real fine job, you and I," said Mr. Snyder, taking one last look at the rabbits as they moved out of sight behind the trees.

Rufus nodded.

"You're very quiet today, Rufus. Something on your mind?"

Rufus shrugged.

"You know, I've been thinking," said Mr. Snyder, looking off into the trees. "I can't let a first-rate man with animals disappear back into the fourth grade. So I've been thinking. I've got a shipment of rats and mice coming, and I'll need help taking care of them. What do you say?"

Rufus just stood there.

"Hey, man. What do you say?"

"Okay," said Rufus, and turned away so Mr. Snyder wouldn't see him cry.

That was in December.

January came and went. And February, March, April, and May. Five days out of every week Rufus got a sandwich and a carton of milk and brought his lunch to Nathaniel Snyder's room. There, side by side, they worked. And talked. There wasn't a word that Mr. Snyder ever spoke to him that Rufus didn't remember. He would never forget.

Up above, the summer sky stretched flat and blue and empty, except for the sun. *Nope,* thought Rufus as he waved a mosquito away from his face, *there won't never be another teacher like Nathaniel Snyder.* And he swiveled around on the stump to give the sun a chance to beat on his back for a while.

In the distance he saw two small shapes moving slowly, one behind the other, back and forth in the red clay furrows between the beds of cotton stalks. The shape in front was Jackson the Mule. The shape behind, guiding the plow, was Rufus's father. Rufus couldn't ever remember a time his father had not been behind the plow.

Long ago, when he was little, Rufus had wanted his father, just once, to draw him close and hold him tight. But his father never had. He had never heard his father laugh either.

The one and only time he had ever seen his father cry was in the late afternoon of the same day he had met Nathaniel Snyder.

All the way home on the bus that October afternoon, Rufus couldn't keep himself still. He tapped his
feet on the floor of the bus and twisted and squirmed
in his seat. The bus crawled along like a snail, making
so many stops, Rufus thought he would leap out a window. He wanted to shout to the driver, "Hurry, man.
Hurry!" But he just jiggled his legs, rocked backward
and forward and kept his mouth clamped shut.

Jimmy Allen leaned over the seat in front. "Quit
your kickin', Rufus. You should of gone to the toilet
'fore we left school." Rufus tuned him out of his mind.

"Your stop, Rufus," the driver called out. Rufus
banged down the aisle, jumped off the bus, and lit out
at a dead run along the path for home.

"Wait'll I tells them," Rufus panted. "Wait'll I
tells them 'bout Nathaniel Snyder an' the rabbits. I ain't
sorry 'cause I love animals. An' I ain't lazy neither.
Nathaniel Snyder do it, an' he be a teacher, too."

Up the path he raced, till he thought his heart
would burst. Up onto the porch he stumbled and into
the room he crashed. *Bang* went the screen door.

Rufus sucked in his breath and stood still as stone.
His father sat in his chair by the table, one hand cupping
the side of his head. And out of each eye and down over
his cheeks flowed two thin streams of tears. His mama

32

was sitting there, too, her ample back to the door. They hadn't stirred since he came in. Didn't even know he was there.

"Sharecroppin' an' me is done for, Anna. I can't go on no more."

"We been makin' it, U.L. It ain't no life, but we been makin' it." His mama reached out a soft hand and covered the rough, gnarled fingers of her man.

"I be goin'," Rufus said under his breath as he backed up to and out the door. He wanted to run to the hog shed and cry there himself. But his legs took him as far as the top step of the porch, then sat him down right within earshot of what was being said inside.

"No more corn. Can't plant no more corn. That's what Mr. Winthrup say. So how we gonna make it?"

"We only plants enough to feed the hogs an' chickens, U.L."

"Woman, you ain't listenin'. No more corn."

"What we gonna do, U.L.?"

"I need that boy, Anna. I need him bad. One man can't make it alone in them fields."

"U.L., that boy don't go into no fields. You know that, so why you ask? What you thinkin' of? You put that boy out in them fields an' God gonna come down an' take him same as he did the other."

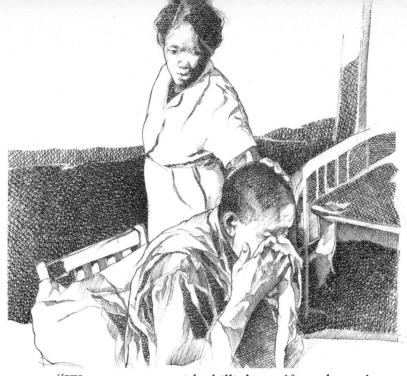

"Woman, woman. I be killin' *myself* out there, day after day. An' he be sittin' all the while in that school doin' nothin'."

"He's learnin', U.L."

"Learnin' what? How to plant cotton? Nossir. He's sittin' there, learnin' how to do nothin'."

"U.L., I los' one child to you out in them fields. An' I don't intends to lose another. God was a-tellin' us. He mean for somethin' better for Rufus."

"Don't talk God to me, woman. God ain't the one out by hisself in them fields. God ain't the one puttin' food in your mouth an' the boy's."

"It's God who's watchin' over us, U.L. He ain't gonna let you die no more'n he's gonna make Rufus quit school. The boy's the one thing we got left."

G 1573477

So here I be, thought Rufus. *Sittin' out in a field, doin' nothin'—'cept bein' with animals. An' I been with them all my life. 'Ceptin' now it's different.*

Thinking back on it, Rufus couldn't be sure which animal he had gotten to know first. But it must have been Jackson the Mule. He'd known Jackson four years come next spring.

There had been other mules. Lots of them. But they all stayed over to Mr. Winthrup's. Sometimes, at the end of a day, his father had given him a boost up onto the back of a mule and the three of them had taken it slow back to Mr. Winthrup's. And while his father and Mr. Winthrup talked business, he watched the boys bed the mules down for the night. Then along came Jackson.

Of course, he would never have gotten to know Jackson, except for the far distance between Mr. Winthrup's farm and the fields Rufus's father now worked. Too far to keep getting him in the morning and bringing him back at night. So his father and Mr. Winthrup made an arrangement. His father would keep Jackson on his place and Mr. Winthrup would supply the feed.

Rufus had been helping his mama weed their kitchen garden. It was a small patch out behind the shack with one old live oak tree to give it shade. He had been traveling on his hands and knees most of an hour down the rows of collard greens, mustard greens, turnips, black-eyed peas, sweet potatoes, and sweet corn, pulling up as many grubs as tough-rooted weeds. And he had about had enough, when across the fields came his father with a bone-thin, swaybacked mule in tow.

Rufus left off weeding in a hurry, to have a closer look at the mule. He was the sorriest-looking mule Rufus had ever seen.

"He look old an' wore out, but he's sound," said his father.

Rufus laid a hand on the withers and felt the mule's skin quiver to his touch. There were long welts on the mule's rump and open sores on its back where the harness had rubbed raw.

"Take him, boy. Bed him down. Mr. Winthrup be along in the mornin' with a salt lick an' some mash."

Rufus took the long plow reins and led the mule into the tumbledown shed. As soon as they heard him coming, the hogs began a fearful racket, grunting and squealing to get Rufus's attention, and the mule's eyes got as round as saucers. "Don't pay them no mind," Rufus told the mule. "They be bigmouthed hogs is all. They don't mean you no harm. You stay here nice an' quiet, while I fixes up the stall."

He hitched the mule on the far side of the shed away from the hogs' pen and got busy carting out the hoes and shovels, pronged spades and pitchforks that were stored in the walk-in stall. He swept the floor and wall boards clean, then got a sickle and went into the fields to cut some hay. Fluffed up and spread out, the hay made a sweet-smelling bed for the mule. In one corner of the stall, Rufus left a pile of green grass and clover. He hung a bucket of water nose-high on a hook in the other corner, then walked the mule into the stall. He slid off the harness, slipped on an old rope halter, and tied the mule secure.

"I still gotta get you somethin' for your sores. Gotta make you fit." Rufus crossed the yard, went into the shack, and was soon back in the stall with the ointment his mama used for burns.

"Now this won't hurt none. So don't be jumpin' around, hear?" Rufus got a couple of fingers full of salve and began spreading it over the sores. "See, that don't hurt, do it? You gonna be well fast, so fast you won't never know you was sick. Tomorrow, 'fore you go out, I'll put some more stuff on an' get some cotton to go under the straps."

Rufus had to stand on tiptoe to reach the mule's back. And every time he stretched up, he waited for the

mule to stomp on his bare toes or to push him hard against the splintery boards. But the mule just hung its head low and blew into the hay.

"They sure whup the spunk outta you. I gets whuppins, too, sometime. They sure be mean . . . They sure be mean," Rufus said softly into the blackness of the shed. The sun had long since set. There was no more seeing in the shed. Only the noises of the hogs and the sweet, thick smell of mule, stayed.

That night Rufus couldn't get to sleep. He lay awake trying to think of a name for the mule. He wanted to call him something fine. At last he decided. He'd call him Jackson. Jackson Gideon Grant. He didn't think his mama would be too pleased. He'd have to keep the name a secret, just between himself and the mule. Jackson had been his brother's name.

The sun, thought Rufus, *never shine cold. Wouldn't like it if it did. Hot sunshine. That's what I like.* And he watched a pair of buzzards circling lazily in the sky. *They prob'ly think I be some ol' dead thing. Sittin' out here so still. But they do fly pretty. On the ground, they be somethin' else again.*

Two days ago, when he came home from school, his father had sent him off to find the sow and her five little piglets. Rufus found them. Dead. In the ditch beside Route 15. They were laid out all in a line just the way they must have been when some speeding car caught them as they tried to cross the road. They weren't long dead. Vultures and buzzards hadn't touched them yet. The birds were gathering, though, high up in the sky. And soon they would settle with a flapping of wings on the fence posts and the ground. They would prance and waddle to the meat. And start to eat.

Rufus turned his back on the pigs. He walked and walked and walked beside the highway, and cried.

I reckon I would of kept on walkin', too, 'cept I seen the magazine. I almost stepped on it, lyin' there, all wet an' ragged in the grass.

Even in the beat-up shape it was in, it was beautiful. It had a bright yellow cover and pages and pages of colored photographs.

Rufus smoothed out the pages, patting them dry on his shirt front. Then he sat down to look at the pictures: pictures of fishes and strange-looking sheep and—he stopped flipping the pages, and stared. There, inside the magazine was this lady, climbing giant trees and playing

with wild chimpanzees. She loved animals, too. He could tell from the pictures. But who was she? And what was she doing living with a bunch of apes? Rufus kept turning the pages till he got to the beginning of the article. There he found the answer. The lady was a "scientific zoologist."

Rufus took the magazine home, and out in the cool dark of the hog shed he studied the pictures and read the story about this lady, over and over again. What was a *zoo-lo-gist?* He would ask Mr. Snyder, tomorrow. Mr. Snyder would know.

That were yesterday. Only yesterday that I learned all about it. Seem like a year. Time go so slow out here. But it were yesterday. That be a hot day, too. Like today. And Rufus sat on the stump, feeling the trickles of sweat slide down the sides of his face and down the backs of his legs. On his arms, tiny beads of sweat caught the sunlight and made his arms glisten like the feathers on the wings of a crow. *Yesterday . . .*

As soon as he climbed up the steps and into the school bus for the long ride home, he met the heat— the heavy, lifeless heat of closed-up places that made him gulp for air. But yesterday he never once thought about the trapped feeling he always got when he entered the bus. There, sitting in the very first seat was Mr. Snyder, and the seat next to his was empty.

"Mr. Snyder, I been lookin' for you all day!"

"Rufus. I was trying to find you, too. Sit yourself down." Rufus plopped into the seat, and while Mr. Snyder loosened his tie and unbuttoned the top button of his starched white shirt, Rufus reached under his T-shirt and carefully withdrew the yellow magazine.

"I found it," said Rufus.

"What have you found?" asked Mr. Snyder, mopping his brow with one of his large white handkerchiefs.

"The thing I'm gonna be. It say it all here, right inside this magazine."

Mr. Snyder leaned over Rufus's shoulder for a closer look.

"That's a good magazine, Rufus."

"It sure is, an' it say all this stuff about this thing."

"What thing is that?"

"The thing I got to ask you about. Here 'tis," said Rufus. He had opened to the story about the lady and

was pointing to the word. "What's a *zoo-lo-gist*?"

"That's zo-ah-lo-jist," said Mr. Snyder.

"Zo-ah-lo-jist," repeated Rufus. "What is it?"

"Zoologist means someone who studies animals—what they look like, what they eat, how they behave."

"Can anyone be this zoologist?"

"Sure."

"Do a zoologist spend most of his time outside?"

"He has to. Most of the animals he studies are living outside, free and wild."

"That's for me," said Rufus. "That's for me. An' what about boys. Can a boy be a zoologist?"

"Can't see why not. You know, Rufus, I think you'll make a great zoologist."

"I been thinkin' 'bout it."

The bus bounced along and the two of them sat silent for a time. Then suddenly, Mr. Snyder practically leapt out of his seat.

"I've got it. I've got a great idea. Now you listen, Rufus, and listen good. If you're going to be a zoologist, you can't waste a minute. I've got some books I'll send you. We can write back and forth. And you can practice doing field work this summer."

For a second, Rufus, had an uneasy picture of himself hoeing a bean patch. But then Mr. Snyder explained.

"You pick a spot—out in the fields somewhere—and you sit there quietly, and watch. Take along some paper and a pencil and make notes of every animal you see. Write down what they look like, what they eat, and what they do. If you keep very still and are very patient, you might see an animal do something that no one else has ever seen it do."

"That truth, Mr. Snyder?"

"That's truth, Rufus."

All last night he had lain awake, thinking about the things he and Mr. Snyder had talked about on the bus. Had talked about almost every day since that morning back in October. So many things about himself began to make sense. *There weren't nothin' wrong with me. I been a zoologist all along. Just didn't know it is all. Now I got me somethin' they can be proud of me for.* And he lay there on the outermost edge of the bed, wishing it would hurry up and be morning.

Doing something for fun and doing it for serious were two different things. He knew that. It was not going to be easy to become a real zoologist. He was going to have to read and study a lot of books and take a lot of notes. It might even be hard work, like now, for instance. Here he was, the first day out in the fields on the job, and he was melting away like a piece of ice.

The longer he sat on the tree stump, the wetter he got, and the lumpier his pants pockets became. He never went into the fields with his pockets empty. But today he had brought along some extras—one spiral pad, two pencils—that added their bulges to the regular pocketfuls of corn kernels, a small salt lick, two empty match boxes, and an old baby bottle filled with water. He hoped his mama hadn't missed the baby bottle; she sometimes used it to sprinkle the wash.

"You sure be a scorcher," Rufus told the sun. From where he sat at the edge of the field facing south, Rufus figured it was close to noon. The sun sat in the middle of heaven, a white-hot ball of fire shining right in his face. Little by little, all morning long, Rufus had felt the skin on his lips and cheekbones pulling tighter and tighter. And now the muscles at the corners of his eyes ached from squinting, and his eyes began to water.

"Better give 'em a rest else all I'll be seein' is dancin' spots." Rufus closed his eyes. "If I was a tomato, I'd split." Rufus smiled, and his bottom lip cracked. "Ouch!" He licked his lip to get it moist. "If somethin' don't happen soon, Mama'll be ringin' the cowbell and I'll has to quit for the day."

Rufus was still busy licking his lip, when he heard it—a flopping, rustling noise off to his left. He opened his eyes wide, then narrowed them to slits as inch by inch he turned toward the sound. Whatever it was, thrashing about in the tall grass, it had to be small. For even with his sharp, field-trained eyes, Rufus couldn't spot it. So he just sat still and watched and waited. Every now and again, the thing gave off a tiny, high-pitched squeak. *Maybe it's only a field mouse bein' ate by a snake,* Rufus told himself. Then the tall grass stopped waving, and there was silence.

Very slowly, Rufus got up off the stump. His legs were stiff and his seat was sore, but he moved quietly through the dry grass until he stood directly over the place.

A shaft of sunlight filtered through the grass and fell on a patch of reddish fur. The patch of fur trembled.

"Hush, now," crooned Rufus, "whatever you be. It's only me." And he spread apart the grass, gradually working his hands down the long, golden stalks until he reached bare ground.

"Shhh," he whispered. On the ground lay a beautiful fox-red bat.

"Hey!" said Rufus, forgetting to whisper. "What you doin' down here? You suppose to be high in a ol' cypress tree. You gonna fry down here."

The little bat tried to wriggle its over-large wings, but gave up and lay flopped on its side, panting to get cool. Rufus, shifted his body so that he shaded the bat. Then he dug into his back pocket and brought out the baby bottle. He shook a few drops of water on to the tip of his forefinger and brushed his finger across the bat's mouth. Then he waited.

At last, a thin sliver of a red tongue flicked out and licked off the drops of water. Drop by drop Rufus gave the little bat all the water it would drink, until it would drink no more.

"Well, you won't go dry for a while," he told the bat, as he unscrewed the nipple top and gave himself a drink. The water was as warm as puddle water, but it

was wet, and he nearly emptied the bottle. He shook the remaining drops over the bat.

That done, and the baby bottle returned to his pants pocket, Rufus was about to hike the bat back to the bog when the faraway tinkle of the cowbell came, calling him home.

"You hear that? I gotta go . . . Yeah, but I can't let you cook, now can I? Nope. You gonna come home with me." Rufus bent down, gathered the bat into the cup of his hands and headed for home.

He took small, quick steps, taking care to avoid stones, ruts, and burrow holes that would make him stumble or fall.

The bat seemed content. It sat quietly in the palms of his hands and looked up at his face, studying him with its bold, black-button eyes. Rufus looked down into the bat's squashed little face and smiled. He'd never known the feel of a bat before. Its fur was thick and soft as kittens' fur. And its wings were knobby and rubbery. It was a queer mixture with almost no weight to it at all. But the bat was beautiful and smelled of moss and meadow.

Two sparrows swooped across his path, and Rufus brought his head up with a jerk. "Can't daydream now. Gotta watch where I'm goin'." One of the sparrows

caught a white moth, and the other sparrow gave chase.
Then both birds disappeared, one after the other, into
the tall grass.

Hey! A thought flashed through Rufus's mind.
That's somethin' to write down. Sparrows eat moths.

He was almost home. The tiny square with the
silvery roof that had looked like a matchbox in the distance now rose wooden and gray, tarpapered and
patched, just up ahead.

Wisps of cooking smoke drifted out the top of
the tin stove-chimney. Rufus's mama stood behind the
screen door, watching for him.

"You late, Rufus. Your papa gonna be mad."

"Yes 'um," said Rufus. And while his mama fin-
ished filling the small pails of soup and coffee for his
father's lunch, Rufus hunted around in the small room
for a place to hide the bat. *The shelf? No. The table?
No. The bed? Yes!* Rufus crossed the room and quickly
hung the bat upside down from the crisscross spring
section underneath the mattress.

"It's ready."

"Yes 'um."

"An' don't dawdle, hear?"

"Yes 'um." Rufus nudged the screen door open with his elbow and, balancing the hot pails by their slender handles, got clear of the door, dodged a couple of chickens and made it safely out to the acre his father and Jackson were plowing.

"Here 'tis," said Rufus. "It's real hot."

His father was sitting on a large rock, waiting and fanning himself with his old straw hat. He took the two pails without a nod or a word.

While his father sat on the rock, drinking his steaming lunch, Rufus unharnessed the mule and led him to the pasture to graze. When they arrived at the green grasses, every step they took sent up clouds of tiny insects. Jackson spent more time sneezing and blowing the bugs out of his nostrils than he did cropping the sweet moist shoots. And sometimes his big soft lips brushed over the tops of Rufus's bare feet as the mule nibbled and stepped, nibbled and stepped his way across the field.

When Rufus brought Jackson back, he found his
father bent over the blade of the plow, scraping it clean.
As soon as Jackson was hitched up again, Rufus's father
slapped the mule on the rump with the reins. "Aiee
yup," he said half to himself. Rufus watched his father
and Jackson the Mule take up where they'd left off on
their slow rutted journey back and forth, up and down,
under the sun.

For Rufus, the rest of the day went as usual. He carried the empty pails back to his mama—he was glad to see she had not found the bat. Then he mucked out the mule's stall. He slopped the hogs. And then he spent what seemed hours, taking down the dry wash and folding it neat and smooth the way his mama wanted it.

The sun set while he was collecting the eggs. Dusk moved in as he stood among the chickens, saucepan in hand, tossing them fistfuls of grain seed and corn kernels.

Rufus stopped once to sniff the air. Out through the screen door came the smell of something special cooking. Corn bread. Rufus felt his mouth flood with saliva. He was so hungry. Then he remembered. He hadn't eaten anything since supper the night before. His stomach gave a great rumbling growl.

He banged the saucepan empty against his thigh, and was just saying to himself that he wished his father and Jackson would hurry-up home, when the two of them appeared from behind the shed. His father dropped the knotted reins over Jackson's withers and walked straight to the shack.

Rufus drew the reins over Jackson's head, as he did every night, and led him into the barn, into the stall which he had cleaned and freshly bedded with hay. He fetched Jackson a bucket of clear water. And while the mule took deep, slurping draughts, Rufus gave him a long, tight hug.

At last. The chores were done and it was time for supper. Rufus hastily rinsed his hands, then stuck his head under the water pump. He was ready to eat a bear.

Inside, the first thing he saw was the big platter of

sun-yellow corn bread right in the middle of the table. Then he saw the lighted kerosene lamp and the regular party of moths and mosquitoes and gnats that danced in its glow. *Maybe tonight, at supper, I can tell them 'bout my plans—'bout the thing I been all along an' am gonna be when I grows up. Maybe.*

His father sat at the head of the table; his mama sat facing him, dishing out the beans and grits. Rufus sat down between them, facing the platter of corn bread.

" 'Lord, bless this food . . . An' them that eats it," said his mama.

"A-men," said his father.

"Amen" was the signal to begin. Rufus reached out a hand to get a piece of corn bread—but that's as far as he got. A sudden whirring stirred the air. The flapping of wings and a series of piercing *eep-eep* sounds filled the room.

The bat!

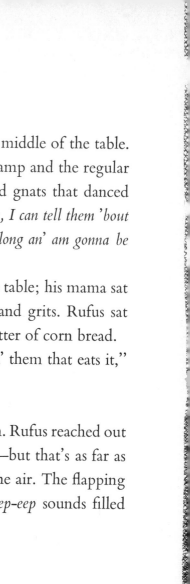

In an instant, his mama had the broom by the handle. Rufus stole a quick look at his father. His father went right on with his eating. A few good swats and the beautiful red bat was pinned to the floor near the door. Rufus's mama opened the door. "Shoo," she said, and with a whisk of the broom she swept the bat out into the night.

"Now," she demanded, "how did that dirty ol' bat get in here? Rufus?" She was looking right at him.

"Yes 'um?"

"Rufus, did you bring that thing in here?"

"Yes 'um."

"Whatever for?"

"Because . . ." Rufus began, his chin digging into his chest.

A chair scraped against the floor boards. His father pushed aside his empty platter and fixed Rufus with stony eyes. "Anna, can't you see this boy is no damn good? His place is behin' a plow," he said, his voice hard and angry.

"No, U.L., no," said his mama. "The boy's not bad. He still be a child is all."

Rufus sat in his chair, slouched and tense, and listened. He wished both of them would quit and leave him alone.

"U.L., someday this child's gonna make us proud. I can feel it inside."

His father said no more. He went to the bed and lay down with his back to the room. Rufus began to shiver, and his mama came to him and put her arms around him and squeezed him to her.

"Rufus, child, why did you do it?"

"Because...because," said Rufus, "I'm a zoologist."

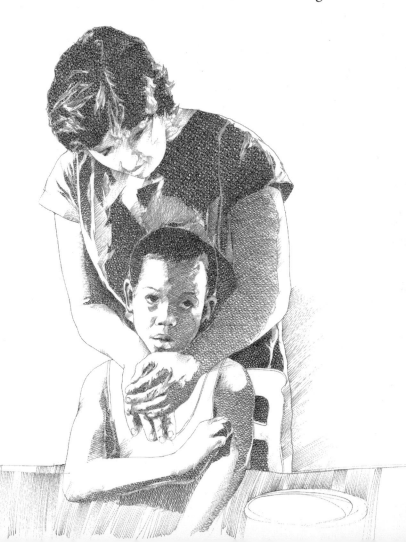